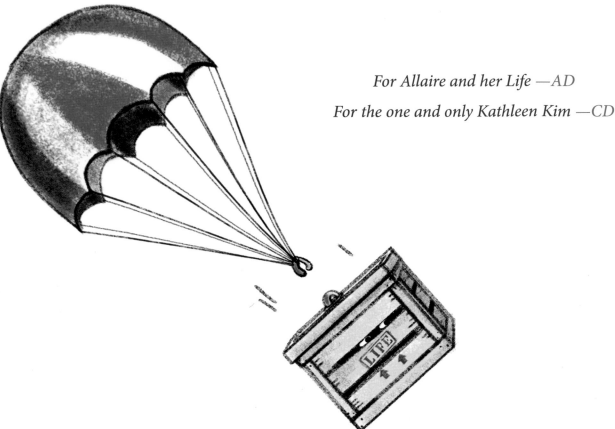

For Allaire and her Life —AD

For the one and only Kathleen Kim —CD

ABOUT THIS BOOK

The illustrations for this book were done in digital paint. This book was edited by Mary-Kate Gaudet and designed by Véronique Lefèvre Sweet. The production was supervised by Bernadette Flinn, and the production editor was Marisa Finkelstein. The text was set in Monkton, and the display type is Paltime Marquee.

THAT'S LIFE!

Written by **AME DYCKMAN**

Illustrated by **CORI DOERRFELD**

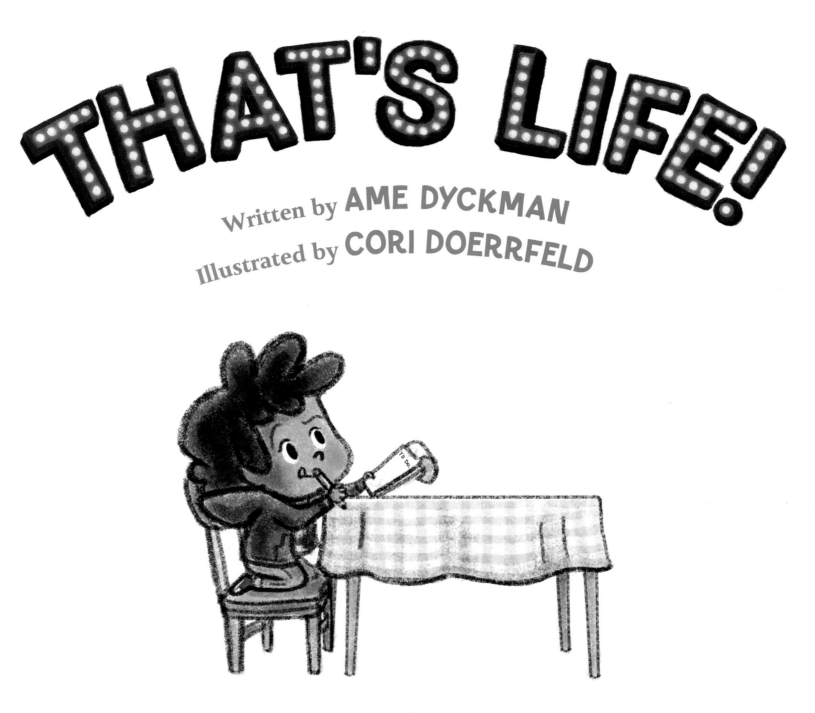

Little, Brown and Company

New York Boston

Who could that be?

Oh, that's Life! Life happens when you least expect it.

Go on! Take a look at your Life!
Just brace yourself. Life can be a little…

And Life doesn't come with instructions.
You hafta write your own.

But—

Life doesn't wait!

You never know where
Life's gonna take you.

Or what Life's gonna throw at you.

But Life is what
you make it!

Life's a journey,

not a destination.

Right when you think you
have Life all figured out…

YOU DON'T!
Life is full of surprises.

When Life knocks you down…

get back up.

When Life stinks…

shake it off. Life will be sweet again.

When Life gives you lemons—

Very funny, Life.

(Life has a sense
of humor.)

Sure, Life can be tough.

And sometimes…

Life hurts!

Call it a Life Lesson.

Life goes on.

So go on after it!

Don't waste a second.

Life is short, but—

CRASH!

Life, uh…finds a way.

And Life. Gets. **MESSY!**

When you need to clean up your Life,
Life doesn't always cooperate.

Your whole Life can flash before your eyes.

Yes, Life can be **CRAZY!**

You might not know what
you're gonna do with your Life!

But when Life finally settles down,
you can appreciate Life for what it is:

Life is

Beautiful!

Still weird. But beautiful.

So love your Life! 'Cause when you do...

your Life
will love you back.

Have the time
of your Life!